Gandhi

A MARCH TO THE SEA

by **Alice B. McGinty**   illustrated by **Thomas Gonzalez**

AMAZON CHILDREN'S PUBLISHING

Mohandas Gandhi once said, " . . . it is not enough to be good. We must also be brave and at the same time have wisdom."

As a child, Gandhi had many fears. He was so afraid of the dark that he slept with a light on. He was loving and strong-willed, however, and wise enough to know right from wrong.

Gandhi thought that solving problems with violence was wrong. It was also wrong, he believed, for his country, India, to be ruled by Great Britain. The British passed unfair laws, such as one that didn't allow Indians to take salt from the sea. Instead, the Indians had to buy salt from the British and pay high taxes on it. Because of this, most Indians could barely afford to salt their food. Taxes on salt and cloth and land made the British rich and the Indians poor.

Gandhi wanted to free India from British rule. As an adult, he organized non-violent protests to challenge the British laws. He called his movement Satyagraha, meaning "soul force."

Among Gandhi's peaceful protests was his famous March to the Sea.

"Next to air and water, salt is perhaps the greatest necessity of life."

—GANDHI
INDIA, 1930

JUST BEFORE SUNRISE,
a small, brown-skinned man
takes a step toward the salty sea
many miles away.
With over seventy marchers,
Mohandas Gandhi begins his journey.

Thousands of Indians,
hungry and poor,
crowd the marchers,
crying farewells,
praying their countrymen
will win the fight
for freedom
and a better life,
as they march to break a law.

British officers
mix with the crowd,
watching every move.
Worries rumble. Rumors brew.

Will Gandhi be arrested?
Will the marchers go to jail?
Are there machine guns
stationed down the road?

Gandhi takes the lead
with his walking stick,
his steps fast and firm.
The marchers rush
to keep the pace,
and praise their God in song:
Ragu-pati Raag-av, Raaja Raam

Every man is ready
to walk this risky road.
Each stride they take,
each law they break:
Peaceful steps toward freedom.

Harsh sun, salty sweat
drips down dusty backs.
Turbaned dancers
lead the marchers
to a shady place to rest.

Gandhi, once a quiet child,
once a lawyer
too shy to talk,
sits high before the villagers
and speaks out, soft but clear.

A law forbidding Indians
from taking salt from the sea—
he tells them this is wrong.
So are the taxes
on the salt they buy,
and on high-priced cloth for clothing.

Gandhi has taught the villagers
to spin their own yarn for clothing.
Now he vows,
" . . . we shall prepare salt,
eat it, sell it to the people . . ."
They know they may
be sent to jail.

They'll pay no more unfair taxes,
follow no more unfair laws.

Each law broken, every stride,
every garment spun,
every Indian who joins the fight:
One more step toward freedom.

Dusty roads, sandaled feet
march each day by dawn,
crossing cotton fields and rivers,
village to village to town.

Flags wave, banners fly,
crowds cheer at the village square.
But this time Gandhi
marches by.

He finally stops,
at the far edge of town,
where the Untouchables live.
Outcasts of the Hindu faith,
dirty, ragged, poor,
pushed away by all—
but Gandhi.

With his own hands,
Gandhi draws water,
from the Untouchables' well,
to wash his dusty body
cool and clean.

Disgust and fear
brew like storms
in the villagers' watching eyes.
Gandhi responds
with a warm, sure gaze.

To treat other Indians
as less than equal,
like the British have treated them?

He tells Muslims, Hindus, and Untouchables
that they are different but the same.
India needs them all
to work as one
for freedom.

Each law broken, every stride,
every garment spun,
every Indian who joins the fight,
each voice raised for what is right:
One more step toward freedom.

After a short night's sleep,
Gandhi rises in the moonlight,
writing letters
and waking his marchers to pray:
        Muslims, a Christian,
        Hindus like himself,
        and Untouchables, too.

A family,
praying together,
spinning yarn,
fighting together for what is right,
for a better life.

The marchers grow weary,
worried, and sick.

Village crowds grow small.

Will enough countrymen
join the fight
to make their country free?

Long wooden bridges
over marshy land
lead the marchers to the sea.
The Arabian Sea—
white salt dusting dark sand.

The next morning,
Gandhi bathes
in the rough, warm waves
and walks to a hollow
in the muddy ground.

He and his marchers
look up to see
a crowd of thousands
gathered:

Indians with eager hearts,
journalists ready
to send stories to the world,
wondering if this small man
leading this big fight
can make things right.

With thin fingers,
Gandhi scoops up
the salty, sandy mud.
He holds out the pile
for all to see. Salt!

All around India,
a door opens:
Hundreds of thousands
—Hindus, Muslims, and Untouchables,
in villages, cities, and towns,
scoop salt from the sea,
boil it,
clean it,
sell it,
buy it,
sprinkle it.

They are arrested,
sent to jail,
until the prisons overflow,
and the British let them go.

Never has salt tasted sweeter.

Each law broken, every stride,
every garment spun,
every Indian who joined the fight,
each voice raised for what was right:
One great man led India
step by step to freedom.

ROUTE OF THE SALT MARCH

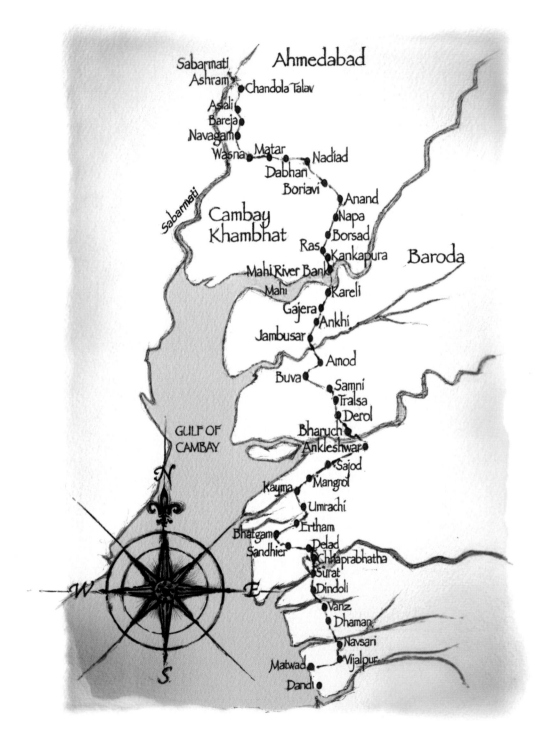

On the day that Gandhi and his marchers reached the sea, Gandhi said, *"In all humility but in perfect truth I claim that if we attain our end through non-violent means India will have delivered a message for the world."* The next morning, on April 6, 1930, he scooped salty mud from the beach, breaking the law.

Gandhi did deliver a message for the world. His twenty-four day March to the Sea received international press coverage. It caught the attention of India's people and many of them joined the Satyagraha movement. They broke the salt laws, made and sold homemade cloth, and worked to form a strong Indian government.

For the next seventeen years, Gandhi and his followers protested peacefully to free India from British rule. Gandhi worked to make peace between the Hindus and Muslims, who battled each other bitterly. He fasted to support the Untouchables' right to elect members to the Indian Government.

In 1947, Gandhi finally achieved his dream. India became free after almost 200 years of British rule. Gandhi and his non-violent movement have been an inspiration to leaders everywhere.

SOURCE NOTES

"It is not enough to be good..." Speech at Prayer Meeting, New Delhi, September 19, 1947, *Collected Works of Mahatma Gandhi*, (Publications Division, Ministry of Information and Broadcasting, Gov't of India, 1971) Vol. 96, p. 391. Hereafter cited as Collected Works.

"Next to air and water, salt is perhaps the greatest necessity of life." *Young India*, February 27, 1930, Vol. 48, pp. 349-50.

"...we shall prepare salt, eat it, sell it to the people..." Speech at Aslali, March 12, 1930, *Collected Works*, Vol. 43, p. 63.

"In all humility but in perfect truth..." Gandhi's Message to America, Dandi, April 5, 1930, *Collected Works*, Vol. 43, p. 180.

ADDITIONAL BOOKS CONSULTED

Gandhi, Mohandas K. *Gandhi: An Autobiography. The Story of My Experiments with Truth.* Boston, MA: Beacon Press, 1957.

Gandhi, Rajmohan. *Mohandas: A True Story of a Man, his People, and an Empire.* New Delhi, India/New York, NY: Viking, 2006.

Weber, Thomas. *On the Salt March: The Historiography of Gandhi's March to Dandi.* HarperCollins Publishers, India. 1997, p. 40.

Text copyright © 2013 by Alice B. McGinty
Illustrations copyright © 2013 by Thomas Gonzalez

All rights reserved.
Amazon Publishing
Attn: Amazon Children's Publishing
P.O. Box 400818, Las Vegas, NV 89140
www.amazon.com/amazonchildrenspublishing

Library of Congress Cataloging-in-Publication Data
available upon request.

ISBN-13: 9781477816448 (hardcover)
ISBN-10: 1477816445 (hardcover)
ISBN-13: 9781477866443 (eBook)
ISBN-10: 1477866442 (eBook)

The illustrations are rendered in mixed media consisting
of pastels, watercolors, color pencils and ink.
Book design by Anahid Hamparian
Editor: Margery Cuyler

Printed in China (R)
First edition
10 9 8 7 6 5 4 3 2 1